STICK OUT YOUR TONGUE

Ma Jian left Beijing for Hong Kong in 1987.
After the handover of Hong Kong he moved to
Germany and then London, where he now lives.
His acclaimed book *Red Dust* won the Thomas
Cook Travel Book Award in 2002.

ALSO BY MA JIAN

Red Dust
The Noodle Maker

MA JIAN

Stick Out Your Tongue

TRANSLATED FROM THE CHINESE BY
Flora Drew

VINTAGE BOOKS
London

Published by Vintage 2007

2 4 6 8 10 9 7 5 3 1

Copyright © Ma Jian 1987
Translation copyright © Flora Drew 2006

Ma Jian has asserted his right under the Copyright,
Designs and Patents Act, 1988 to be identified as the author
of this work

First published in Great Britain in 2006 by
Chatto & Windus

Vintage
Random House, 20 Vauxhall Bridge Road,
London SW1V 2SA

www.randomhouse.co.uk/vintage

Addresses for companies within The Random House Group Limited
can be found at: www.randomhouse.co.uk/offices.htm

The Random House Group Limited Reg. No. 954009

A CIP catalogue record for this book
is available from the British Library

ISBN 9780099481331

The Random House Group Limited makes every effort
to ensure that the papers used in its books are made from
trees that have been legally sourced from well-managed and
credibly certified forests. Our paper procurement policy
can be found at: www.randomhouse.co.uk/paper.htm

Printed and bound in Great Britain by
Cox & Wyman Limited, Reading, Berkshire

Contents

For Nannan

The woman and the blue sky

Our bus ground to the top of the five-thousand-metre Kambala Pass. Behind us, a few army trucks were still struggling up the foothills. As the last clouds tore from the rocks and prayer stones on the summit and slipped down the gullies, Yamdrok Lake came into view. When the surface of the lake mirrored the blue sky and plunged the distant snow peaks head-first into the water, I was filled with a sudden longing to take someone in my arms. This was the mountain road to Central Tibet.

During the month that I'd stayed in Lhasa, I had visited many ancient monasteries and shrines, but it was to the Jokhang Temple that I'd returned most frequently. The Jokhang is Tibetan Buddhism's most venerated site. Pilgrims from every corner of Tibet circle its walls in a continual stream, spinning prayer wheels, praying for an end to their suffering in this life and a prosperous rebirth in the next. Crowds prostrate themselves before the entrance, resembling professional athletes as they hurl themselves to the ground, stand up with hands clasped in prayer, then throw themselves down again. These displays of religious fervour appeal to foreign travellers, but sky burials arouse an even greater interest. While I was staying in Lhasa, I trekked to the burial site several times, camera in hand. But I never managed to see a burial: it would either be finished by the time I'd arrived, or relatives of the deceased would spot me from afar and tell me to stay away. Sometimes they even threw stones at me. I always ended up traipsing back to Lhasa in a bad mood.

I had been told that when a Tibetan dies, the relatives keep the body at home for three days, then carry it to the burial site, making sure not to look behind them as they walk. When they reach the village gates or a crossroads, they smash an earthenware jar onto the ground to ensure that the dead person's soul will never return. At the funeral site, the burial master lights a fire of fragrant juniper branches. Wealthy families employ a lama to recite from the scriptures and relate to the guardians of the Buddha Realm the merits and achievements of the deceased. Depending on the level of these achievements, the deceased will either return to the world of men, or remain in the Buddha Realm for eternity. The burial master hacks all the flesh from the corpse and slices it into small pieces. He grinds the bones into a fine powder and adds some water to form a paste. (If the bones are young and soft, he will thicken it with ground barley.) He then feeds this paste, together with the flesh, to the surrounding hawks and vultures. If the deceased was a Buddhist, a holy swastika will be carved on the corpse's back. When everything has been eaten, the master presents the scalp to the relatives, and the burial is considered to be complete. After that, the only way the relatives can communicate with the deceased is to go to the temple and pray.

I was travelling to the remote countryside of Central Tibet. When the bus reached the foot of the mountain and hurtled along the shores of Yamdrok Lake, I began to feel dizzy. I opened the window. The lake was calm; there wasn't a speck of dust in the breeze. The bus, however, was crammed to the brim, and the stench of dank sheepskin that wafted from the back made it hard for me to breathe. When I could take it no longer, I told the driver to stop, and jumped out.

It was August. The Tibetan Plateau's golden month. The sky was so blue and transparent, it felt as though there was no air. I walked to the shore of the lake, put down my bag, took out a flannel and washed my face. In the distance, at the foot of a mountain, I could see the village of Nangartse. A hundred or so mud houses stood in rows along the foothills, prayer flags jutting from each roof. Above them, halfway up the mountain, was a small Buddhist temple, its walls painted in strips of red and white with a band of blue running below the eaves. Beside it were the ruins of a monastery, and a freshly white-washed stupa, housing the ashes of a dead saint, gleaming in the sun.

It was a beautiful place. The shores of the lake were clean. The water was so clear, I could see every pebble. Beams of sunlight shone right down to the bed. The coloured prayer flags on the distant roofs moved in the wind, whispering the beauty of the Buddha Realm. Below the houses, near the shore of the lake, stood a cement hut with a red tiled roof. I assumed it was the village headquarters, and pulled out from my bag a forged introduction letter that was stamped with a red seal. As I approached, I discovered that it was not the village headquarters, it was just an ordinary brick hut. A soldier stepped out. From his accent I could tell that he was from Sichuan. He invited me to come inside and sit down, so I followed him through the door. The hut was an army repair station. The soldier had been posted here to maintain the smooth connection of the army telephone line. When the line was working, he would go fishing on the lake, and read a few kung-fu novels too, I assumed – seeing the pile of them lying on the floor. He was delighted when I asked to stay. He had lived here for four years, and could speak Tibetan quite well. He often went up to the village to have a drink with the locals. A rifle hung from a nail on the wall. The room was a mess – it looked like a scrap yard.

I asked if there was a burial site nearby, and he said that there was. Then I asked if there had been any burials lately. He froze for a second, and told me that a woman in the village had recently passed away. When I asked whether I might be allowed to watch the burial, the soldier muttered inaudibly then said that he needed to buy some beer. I handed him some money, but he pushed it away and walked out of the door. It occurred to me that this might be my last chance to see a sky burial: I was unlikely to come across one again in the next few days. I couldn't let this opportunity slip by.

In the evening, we opened the beers and chatted about the latest news from China. I tried to worm myself into his favour. He liked to fish, so I said that I liked fishing too, and promised that when I returned to Beijing I would send him an imported, stainless-steel fishing rod. I gave him my address and bragged that Premier Zhao Ziyang lived right next door to me. Needless to say, you could search Beijing for days and never find the address that I scribbled down for him. Then I talked about women. He listened avidly, sucking at his cigarette. I told him wild stories about today's liberated women, and in a Sichuan dialect I assured him that when he came to Beijing, I would let him sleep with my girlfriend. 'No problem,' I said. He brushed his hand over the table, then paused and told me that the woman was only seventeen. I couldn't believe it. So young. 'She died of a haemorrhage during childbirth,' he said. 'The foetus is still inside her womb.'

I crushed out my cigarette. We both fell silent. The floor of the room was damp. A single bed was pushed against the wall. The bed was wooden and painted yellow; on its headboard were a red star and an army regiment number. The walls of the room were pasted with pages torn from colour magazines. A pile of hooks and electric cables lay scattered beneath the washstand behind the door. There was just one window in the room. The lower pane was covered with a sheet of newspaper. Through the upper pane, I watched the sky turn from dark blue to black. It had been a long time since I'd heard a truck pass by outside.

The soldier stood up, leaned against the bed and said, 'You can go to the burial if you like. The people here won't mind. Most of them have never seen a

6

camera before. Myima's two husbands certainly haven't.'

'Whose two husbands?' I asked.

'The dead woman's.'

'How come she had two husbands?'

'She married two brothers, that's why,' he answered quietly.

I paused, then asked why she had married two brothers. But as soon as the question left my mouth, I realised how disrespectful it sounded. The woman was dead. It was no business of mine why she had married two men.

He answered me, though. 'Myima was not from these parts. She was born in Nathula. She was a weak child, the youngest of eleven. When she was six years old, her parents sold her to another family in exchange for nine sheep hides.'

'Does that kind of thing still happen, then?' I asked.

He ignored my question and continued, 'She grew stronger after she moved here. She even attended school in Lungmatse. That was before her adoptive mother died, though.'

'And what was *her* name?' I asked, taking a pen from my bag. It sounded like an interesting story.

'Her adoptive father is a drunk. When he drinks too much he breaks into song and starts grabbing women. Sometimes he grabbed Myima. After his wife died, his behaviour got worse. How could a young girl protect herself against such a brute?' His voice was trembling. I could tell that he was about to swear. When he'd been showing off to me a few minutes earlier, he'd let out a torrent of abuse.

'Bloody bastard! Just wait until I'm out of these army clothes!' His face turned from red to purple, in that surly, stubborn way typical of Sichuan men. I kept quiet and waited for his anger to subside.

He went to the door and checked the direction of the wind. The telephone line was completely still. I finished my beer and circled the room. Although it was summer, the altitude was so high that there were no mosquitoes. The damp air from the lake poured into the room and chilled my bones.

'Will you take me to see the brothers?' I asked.

Without looking round, he grabbed a set of keys and a torch from the table and said, 'Let's go.'

We climbed to the village along dark, narrow passages of mud and brick. The path was rough and bumpy. The straw and dung on the ground flinched back silently as my torchlight fell on them. Behind every wall, I could hear the sound of dogs barking.

The soldier pushed through a gate and shouted a few words of Tibetan at a house with a light at the window. We walked inside.

The men seated around the fire turned and stared

at me, mouths agape. The eldest one stood up and started speaking in Tibetan with the soldier, while the others continued to gawp at me. I took out my lighter and flicked it on, then passed my cigarettes around. In the dark, all I could see was the white of the men's teeth. I flicked the lighter again and let the flame rise. Their jaws slackened. I handed the lighter to the man who was standing up. He took it from me and sat down. Everyone's eyes focused on the lighter. They passed it between them, looking up at me from time to time to exchange a smile. At last I felt that I could sit down. The young man next to me took a chunk of dried mutton from his bag and cut me a piece. I had tasted raw mutton like that in Yangpachen, so I pulled the knife from my belt and took a slice. They seemed pleased, and handed me a bowl of barley wine. It was still green, and there were husks floating on the surface. My mind turned to the dead woman.

The smell of burning dung was suffocating. I glanced around the room. It was as simply furnished as most Tibetan homes: prayer scarves draped over a wooden table, whitewashed walls. To the right of the front door was an opening into a dark chamber. I presumed that this was Myima's room, or a larder, perhaps. Opposite the fireplace was a traditional Tibetan cabinet, and a scroll painting of Yama, Lord of Death, gripping the Wheel of Life in his hands and flashing his ferocious teeth. It was an old painting; its edges were pasted with scraps of coloured paper printed with words from the scriptures.

I guessed that the men were discussing my request to see the sky burial. A few of them were talking in Tibetan and nodding at me. The soldier stood up and gestured for me to follow him. He led me to the chamber and shone his torch on a large hemp sack that was tied at the top with cord and stood on a platform of mud bricks.

'That's her,' he said.

I flashed my torch on the sack. She appeared to be sitting upright, facing the door, her head bowed low. I presumed that the men had had to push her head down before they could tie up the sack.

Back in the soldier's hut, I lay on the bed, eyes wide open, imagining what the woman had looked like. She could sing, like the Tibetan women I'd heard in the forests or high on the mountain paths. At noon, she bound her sheepskin cloak to her waist, and bent down over the fields, her long braids of hair slipping over her ears. I gave her the face of a girl I'd seen on a bus: large red cheeks, small nose, dark-rimmed eyes, a steady gaze. Her neck was soft and pale. As I stood beside her, I could see the dark dip between her breasts tremble with each shake of the bus.

The soldier walked in from his nightly inspection of the telephone line and switched on the light. His face was blank. He lit a cigarette and lay down beside me. Neither of us was in a mood to sleep.

Eventually he spoke. 'I might as well tell you. You'll be gone in a few days. Besides, I can't keep this to myself much longer. The pain is too much.' I propped a pillow against the wall and sat up.

'Myima and I were very close,' he continued. 'That's why I've stayed here so long. Most people would have applied for a transfer years ago. I first met her up on the mountain. I'd climbed up to repair the telephone line two mountains behind. She had let her sheep out and was sitting on the grass. On my way back, I was carrying a large bundle of wire. It weighed a ton. I said hello and sat down beside her. Her dog glanced at me then went back to sleep. It was a hot afternoon. Her sheep had wandered off to graze on a breezy slope. She smiled, then looked at me straight in the eye, without any shame or embarrassment. I told her I worked in the repair station below. She didn't understand me, so I traced my finger along the telephone line to my house at the bottom. She laughed and turned her face to the Kambala Pass. Two trucks were driving up the foothills over there, too far away for us to hear. Myima said that she'd seen me before, and asked why I'd stayed here so long. Her accent was different from the other Tibetans in the village. Before I left her that day, I cut off a long piece of wire and gave it to her as a present. I told her that she could use it to hang out her laundry or to tie things up with.

'After that, I often went up the mountain to see her. She'd be sitting there, waiting for me, with home-made dried mutton and barley wine. Sometimes she made gin for me from dates and mountain pears. I would stay with her until sunset. She was cleaner than most Tibetan girls – I grew to like the smell of mutton and milk on her skin. One day, I stretched my hand out to unfasten the belt of her sheepskin cloak. She didn't push me away, so I put my arm around her. She was the first woman I'd ever touched. After that, as soon as I got close to her, or my hand brushed against her cloak, I'd panic. I could tell that she wanted me to put my hand inside her cloak, but I was too afraid. She told me how her adoptive father kept grabbing her, and how she'd often run away and be too fright-ened to return home. Everyone in the village knew about it. All the young men in the village looked down on her.

'Last year, at about this time of night, she burst in to my room and felt her way to my bed. She had never slept here before . . . We spent the whole night together. In the morning, she pushed me aside and said that she had to leave. I helped her get dressed, then I went back to bed. Before she left, she took off the turquoise necklace she'd worn since she was a child and slipped it under my pillow. It wasn't until the next day that I found out that she'd agreed to marry the two brothers.'

He paused and looked up at me. 'If this gets out, I'm finished. My leaders will kill me.'

I nodded solemnly, and gestured to him that I would keep my lips sealed. That is why, in this story, I refer to him only as 'the soldier'.

He took out the necklace from the drawer. I held it under the lamp and studied it closely. It was a string of agate and red wooden beads, with a large lump of turquoise in the middle. The turquoise was smooth and dark, and still smelt of the woman's milky skin. I thought of her now, sitting in the hemp sack on the platform of mud bricks.

'Did she visit you again after that?' I asked.

'No. After she got married, she was busy with her chores and seldom left the house. The brothers liked her very much, apparently. Whenever they'd had a drink, the villagers would hear Myima yelling late into the night. The younger brother was even seen making love to Myima on his horse as he rode back from Wangdan Temple. Myima was already pregnant by then. The brothers were in their forties. They'd never been married before.'

'Why didn't she visit you again?'

'She did,' the soldier replied. 'I just don't want to tell you everything.'

When I reached the sky burial site, the sun had already risen. This wasn't a large flat boulder jutting from a cliff like the burial site in Lhasa, it was a gravel terrace halfway up the mountain between the foothills and the higher slopes. Dirty ropes hung from metal posts that were jammed into cracks in the ground. Beside them lay rusty knives, two hammers and an axe with a broken handle. The gravel was scattered with scraps of bone, clumps of hair, smashed rings, glass beads and bird droppings dotted with human fingernails. The mountain was silent. Hawks and vultures sat perched on the summit. In the valley below, ribbons of mist rose from Yamdrok and rolled into a single sheet that slowly covered the entire lake. The mist thickened and spread, rising and falling like the chest of a woman breathing, drifting higher and higher until it veiled the blood-red sun. The mist still clinging to the lake trembled slightly, then broke free and floated towards the foothills.

Slowly they emerged from the mist. The elder brother was lugging the hemp sack. I guessed that they couldn't afford to hire a burial master, or that perhaps there were none in the area. The younger brother was carrying a felt bag, a thermos flask and a frying pan. A lama followed behind. I recognised him as the man who'd sat beside me the night before in Myima's home. Clouds of mist billowed behind them.

They smiled at me. The sack was opened and Myima's body was pulled out. She was lying in the foetus position, her limbs bound to her chest. The auspicious swastika that had been carved onto her back had dried and shrunk. When the rope was loosened she flopped to the ground. They tied her head to a metal post and pulled her body straight. She was flat on her back now, her eyes fixed on the sky and the scattering clouds of mist.

The younger brother lit a fire of juniper twigs and sprinkled roasted barley on the flames. The thick smoke rose into the mist. Then he moved to a second fire and dropped a lump of yak butter into a frying pan that was resting on a wooden frame. The elder brother fed dung pats to the two fires and glanced at the mountain summit. The lama sat cross-legged on a sheepskin rug counting rosary beads over an open prayer book. He was sitting close to the flames.

I studied the corpse from a distance, then slowly approached. Her limbs were splayed out as though she were preparing to take flight. Her breasts were paler than the rest of her body and drooped softly to either side of her ribcage. Her belly was swollen, the unborn child still lying inside it. I wondered whether the soldier was the father of the child.

I set the aperture of my camera, adjusted the distance, then squatted down beside her and prepared to take a photograph. In the background were clouds of fog and snow peaks flushed by the rising sun. Through the lens, Myima looked like a little girl. I imagined her arriving at this mountain on horse-back as a child of six, peeping out from under her sheepskin cloak to catch her first glimpse of the Kambala Pass. Years later, when she was up here tending her sheep, she would often gaze at the pass and think about her home in the south.

She looked as though she were asleep. I panned my camera down her body. Soft arms, palms upturned to the sky, a red mole under her breast, smooth thighs. I thought of the soldier's creaking wooden bed and of the two brothers who were now gulping the barley wine. I focused on her feet. The soles were white, the toes tightly clenched. The smallest toes were so short there was no room for nails to grow. I stepped back for a wider view and hit the shutter, but nothing happened. I checked the camera, pressed the button again. It was stuck. My legs gave way. I sat down on the ground, wound back the film and changed the battery. I focused on Myima's face this time and pressed the shutter, but the button seemed to be frozen in place. Then, as I looked up, I noticed the corner of Myima's mouth twitch. It was neither a smile nor a sneer, but her mouth definitely moved.

I stood up. A shriek echoed through my head then vanished with a gust of wind. A bald eagle plummeted through the sky, circled the corpse's head, settled on a rock and ruffled its wings.

I tramped back to the fire. The younger brother reached into his felt bag, scooped out a piece of dung and flung it onto the flames. Then he produced a lump of roast barley and broke me off a piece. I chewed it greedily. There were raisins inside. He brought out some dried mutton and filled the lid of the thermos flask with barley wine. I grabbed it and downed it in one. I wondered whether Myima had prepared the mutton. I looked up at her. Her legs were spread open; a piece of string hung from the wounded flesh between her thighs. I presumed that someone had attached it during her troubled labour in an attempt to wrench the baby out. I dragged my knife through the dried mutton. The brothers smiled at me. I smiled too, perhaps, but my face was turned to the distant snowcaps that were reddening in the sun. The fog had vanished, and in the distance Yamdrok looked as calm as it had done the day before, and as blue as Myima's turquoise.

The elder brother got up, threw some more dung onto the fires, then walked to the lama and poured him some wine. The lama pushed the bowl away and announced that Myima's soul had risen to the sky. The younger brother stood up and took a sharp knife from his pocket. I followed the two brothers to the body. Immediately the sky darkened with vultures that screeched and swirled through the air. The brothers turned Myima's body over, stuck the knife into her buttock and pulled it down, opening up her leg all the way to the sole of her foot. The younger brother hacked off a chunk of thigh and sliced it into pieces. Her right leg was soon reduced to bone. With her belly squashed to the ground, sticky fluid began to trickle from between her thighs. I picked up my camera, set the distance, and this time the shutter closed with a snap.

The vultures surrounded us and fought over the scraps of flesh. A pack of crows landed behind them. Perhaps they considered themselves an inferior species, because not one of them dared move forward. They kept their distance, sniffing the air, waiting for their turn.

The morning sun flooded the burial site with light. The younger brother shooed away the approaching vultures with pieces of Myima's body. I picked up the axe, grabbed a severed hand, ran the blade down the palm and threw a thumb to the vultures. The younger brother smiled, took the hand from me and placed it on a rock, then pounded the remaining four fingers flat and threw them to the birds.

When the elder brother dug his knife into Myima's chin and drew it up her face, I suddenly forgot what she had looked like. While the brothers continued to carve, her eyes remained fixed on the sky above, until every piece of her had vanished from the site.

The elder brother snatched a bunch of Myima's braids that were still tied with red thread, swirled it around the circling vultures and staggered back to the fire. The crows had now joined the vultures at the metal posts, and were picking at the roast barley that had been mashed up with scraps of brain.

I checked my watch. I had been up here for two hours already. It was time to go down. I knew that the soldier was waiting for me in his room. He'd promised that he would borrow a boat in the afternoon and take me fishing on the lake.

The smile of lake drolmula

Sonam dismounted his horse at the foot of a hill that he had ridden past a few hours before. He took a deep breath then softly expelled it. The air smelt of grass and the moist, sun-baked earth. The wind was still blowing from the same direction: rising from the valleys of the Gangdise Mountains, sweeping over the flat wastes then racing onwards to the distant shores of Lake Drolmula. Far away, he could see the lake rippling in the wind, as though some great amphibian dinosaur were breathing below the surface. Reeds swayed by the banks and white saline crystals sparkled along the shallow waters. It was a salt lake. Every year, hundreds of yaks and horses drowned in its briny marshes. He was certain that his family would never choose to set up camp along its shores.

He led the horse forward, then stopped, flung the reins onto the horse's back and started up the hill alone. The grass slope was split open by seams of exposed limestone. The fissures in the stone had been deepened by centuries of rain and snow, leaving a treacherous terrain of ridges and ruts. Horses that ventured up the hill would often trip and injure themselves; smaller animals would fall down the wide cracks and drown in the water that collected below. When Sonam reached the top of the hill, he saw the blue sky floating in the pools of stagnant water that dotted the plain below. He glanced back at his horse. It was still standing where he'd left it. He'd been riding it for almost a month now. It was one of his uncle Kelsang's best horses. He hadn't found the riding easy, though. He was out of practice; his thighs and tailbone were very sore. He had grown up in this region of the high plateau. One year, a severe drought had forced his family to move their camp to this very spot. His youngest sister, Gagal, had fallen into a ditch and died while riding her yak up this hill. He was eleven years old at the time.

He turned towards the lake again and continued walking. The pastures spread before him. In the distance, a swathe of pale grass trembled under the sun. There were no clouds, no tents, no animals. His chest felt empty and hollow.

These high pastures were five thousand metres above sea level. A few hardy shrubs, able to withstand the cold winters, spread their leaves under the warm August sun. Sonam kicked some weeds out of the way, sat down on a rock and glanced back again at his horse. It was stamping its hoofs now and whipping away a swarm of gadflies with its tail. Its stomach was no longer shuddering. The wind has stopped, he thought to himself.

It was a slow horse. When he'd collected it from his uncle, Sonam had taken a saddle from another horse and attached it to its back. A few days ago, the hemp sack that had served as the saddle lining fell off, and since then the wooden saddle had been digging straight into the horse's back. Its skin was raw in places. The horse had been in so much pain that it had often bolted off in fits of agony. Sonam remembered the brown stallion that he rode as a boy. It could jump over the deepest ditches. And the white yak. He hadn't ridden a yak since he'd left home two years ago to go to school in Saga.

His heart tightened when he realised how little of his holiday remained. Five days ago, he had come across Old Tashi's family. Tashi still recognised him. He was very old now and could barely stand up. He asked Sonam what black arts he had studied at school in Saga. Tashi's extended family had pitched their various tents across the meadow, but in the evening everyone gathered in the main tent to hear Sonam speak about the outside world.

Tashi was unable to hear a word that Sonam said. He just kept mumbling on about how he too had travelled to Saga as a young boy, to study the black arts. He said that during his uncle's initiation ceremony, the Living Buddha Danba Dorje ripped out his uncle's eyes, pulled out his tongue, chopped off his hand and offered the severed parts to Avalokitesvara, the Bodhisattva of Compassion. After the ceremony, the uncle returned home and died a few days later. Tashi was then sent to Saga to learn some spells that would allow his family to exact their revenge. He took a herd of yaks with him. In Saga, he found a Buddhist master who was able to tame the wind and make hail fall from the sky. Tashi gave the master his yaks, a silver ornament and a brass incense burner in exchange for a year's board and tuition. The master taught him an incantation for subduing one's enemy, as well as a few less dangerous spells. When Tashi returned home, he used the evil incantation to blind Danba Dorje, then he moved camp to this region of the high pastures.

Tashi's nephew, Dhondup, said that Sonam's family had moved to the south-east a month ago. There was a fertile valley there, apparently, but it was almost a two-week trek away. Dhondup also mentioned that Sonam's sister, Dawa, had grown up a lot recently and was now as pretty as a wild raspberry. 'Everyone who sees her wants to take a bite,' Dhondup said. Those words made Sonam feel very uncomfortable.

Dhondup couldn't explain why Sonam's family had decided to move to the valley. Usually, nomads only went there in the autumn. As the mouth of the valley faced north, in the summer there was no wind and the pastures became infested with wasps and mosquitoes that attacked the nomads' herds. Sometimes, the yaks and sheep became so distraught that they abandoned camp and followed the scent of moist air all the way to the marshes of Lake Drolmula. Dhondup told Sonam that his father was in bad health and could no longer throw a lasso, and that his mother had fallen off a horse a while ago and was unable to do any work. I don't believe him, Sonam thought to himself at the time. My mother has never ridden a yak. Perhaps he's confusing this with the story of Gagal's accident.

A breeze blew from Lake Drolmula. Sonam breathed in deeply. The air had a flat, slightly bitter taste. The sky began to darken and the ground beneath him seemed to pull him down. He kicked his numb legs about and staggered to his feet. It was already two days since he had eaten something. His stomach burned with hunger.

He glanced back and saw that the horse had gone.

When did it run away? he wondered. He remembered that he'd dozed off a few minutes ago, when the wind had changed. I should have brought the horse up here, he said to himself. There's no grass to distract it here, and no gadflies. He walked back down the hill and followed the hoof prints the horse had left in the grass. His legs felt very weak.

When night fell he came to a stop. He opened his mouth, then closed it again. A sudden cold descended on the grasslands. He could still sense where Lake Drolmula was, but he couldn't go there. He'd heard that the lake was the urine of Goddess Tadkar Dosangma, and that on the peak of the mountain behind it, you could see the splashes that she had left behind. He knew that it was dangerous to approach the lake. Nevertheless, he was now clearly walking towards it.

Four months ago, he'd sent a letter to his family telling them that he would visit them during his summer holidays. But when he arrived in Mayoumu last month, he found that the letter was lying still unopened in the village headquarters. The officer in charge told him that his family had moved their herd to the Yara valley in spring. Sonam travelled to Yara, but when he got there, the nomads gave conflicting reports of his family's whereabouts. In the end, he'd decided to follow his uncle Kalsang's advice, and come to look for them here on the hills near Lake Drolmula. When he arrived here five days ago, Old Tashi warned him to stay away from the lake. He said that Goddess Tadkar Dosangma goes there to meet her lover, the Mountain God, and that anyone who sees them making love is doomed to lose their sight.

Last night, Sonam sensed that his family were not far. He reached a hill where a tent had just been removed. The upturned earth was damp and the soil below the fire pit was still dry. He even found the piece of apron that his father used as a saddle lining. The embroidery looked very familiar – he was certain that his mother had stitched it.

He remembered Dawa's coloured apron. She has grown up now, he thought to himself. In fact, she was already quite grown up when he left for Saga two years ago. She would no longer undress in front of him, and would always run ten steps away from him before crouching down to piss. He thought of the smell of sour milk on Dawa's body.

Yesterday, when he reached the hill, he turned round to the black horse and said, 'Look, look! Here they are! That's their yak hair carpet!' He fell to his knees and smelt the earth, then he picked up a sheep's hoof that he presumed his family had tossed from the cooking pot, and turned it in his hands. He looked up and said, 'I've been searching for you for a month. Why are you still sitting down, Dawa? Get up, get up. Come to me! I've bought you shoes, made in Beijing. I'll tell you where Beijing is. There are so many people there. More than all the yaks in Mayoumu. My school in Saga has lots of windows, and stairways that go round and round.' Then he paused and looked around him. The breeze blowing from the grasslands smelt of yak shit and sheep bones. At his feet he saw maggots wriggling through a pat of yak dung. He watched the dung puff up, and then slowly sink again.

Tonight he was standing on the high plateau in the pitch dark, the mosquitoes biting into his face. He walked on for a while and saw pale, mauve ripples drift across the surface of the lake. That's where the Goddess pisses, he muttered. He lay down on the ground and gazed into the distance. The Goddess leaves the lake in the winter to join the Mountain God. The lake is her urine. The shore is rimmed with white crystals. That's where she pisses, over there, over there . . . He closed his eyes and slowly dropped off to sleep.

When he woke again, he found himself bathed in the red light of the morning sun. He wanted to return to his dream. Gradually his mind cleared and he sat up and looked back at the route he had taken. He knew that his food and water had run out, that his horse had run away, and that if he didn't come across any nomads soon he would not survive another day. He rose to his feet. As soon as his legs stood firm, blood rushed to his head and his heart started to beat wildly. He was weak with hunger. The black horse must have escaped down this path yesterday, he thought to himself. The slope isn't steep, and the ditch on the left would have been too wide for it to jump. If the horse had run down here, it would have had the wind in its face. This was the only path it could have taken if it had wanted to escape the gadflies.

He gazed at the lake. It was perfectly still. The white salt crystals lay on the shore like a long prayer scarf. Below him, in the brilliant sunlight, a pool of water sparkled like ice. Mounds of wild herbs carpeted the distant marshes. There was no living creature in sight, not even a fly.

He trudged slowly onwards. When he finally reached the lake, he turned right and began walking along the shore. It was as though he thought that, by doing so, he would eventually come across something. He walked for hours, but all he saw were banks of dry grass poisoned by the saline crystals.

He tried to drink some water from the lake, but the taste was so foul he had to spit it out. A fire burned through his stomach. My piss tastes better than that, he muttered. Then he looked up and saw the lake smiling at him. That's just how Dawa used to smile, he thought to himself.

As the sun began to sink again, he stopped and stood still. The Gangdise Mountains were wrapped in mist. The light on the summits grew clearer, then dwindled, left the mountains and hovered for a moment in the sky. A few seconds later, everything went black.

A gust of wind blew into Sonam's face. When it died, his family suddenly appeared before him. First, he saw the tent, the flickering fire and the cooking pot with the aluminium lid. His mother was standing behind the steam, dropping lumps of yak butter into the pot. He could smell the warm butter tea and fried cheese. Then he saw Dawa, or rather, Dawa saw him. She yelped with joy, raced over to him, dug her head into his chest and slapped his shoulders. He laughed and followed her into the tent.

Inside, nothing had changed. The same yak hides covered the ground. His father was leaning against the central pole, as usual, enjoying the warmth of the fire. The yak butter pouch that his mother had used all her life still hung from the same hook.

Sonam placed beside his father's feet the white bucket that he'd brought with him from Saga. He said that this was the bucket the black horse had run off with. Ngawang, his youngest sister, walked in. She hadn't grown at all, and still had the same foolish smile that she'd worn the time he'd wiped coal dust over her face. Dawa looked down at the fire, broke off a lump from the tea brick and threw it into the pot. Sonam presented her with the bag of fine grain salt that he'd brought with him. She had grown up a lot. As she bent over to take the bag of salt from him, her breasts jerked forward and wobbled a little. Immediately he thought of the school sports field where he played football after lunch. Next to the field was a large pond, and behind that was his school. When you looked at the school reflected in the water, its whitewashed walls seemed very clean.

He pulled off his rucksack. Didn't the black horse run off with this too? he asked himself. He opened the sack and took out a neatly folded shirt wrapped in cellophane and gave it to his mother. His two sisters shrieked with delight. They pounced on the sack and started pulling things out. He told them to wash their hands before they touched anything. His father walked over to take a look. He'd had a lot to drink already, and was as weak as Tashi's nephew had warned. He looked like an old butter churn as he leaned down over the sack. The barley wine in his wooden bowl splashed onto his hands each time he lifted it to his mouth.

Sonam felt a chill run down his back, and moved towards the fire. Although it was summer, at night it got so cold, his legs would go numb. Outside, he could hear the sheep huddling together for warmth, stamping their feet from time to time and clashing horns. The warm steam and the smell of yak dung in the tent slowly seeped into his body. He took a few sips of butter tea and checked the taste. The butter was fresh but the tea hadn't brewed long enough and tasted a little of mould.

He wanted to speak. 'Ask me whatever you like,' he said. 'Have you seen the big building I live in? It's very tall. There are rooms on each floor.' He thought about the cinema near his school and said, 'One day we could all be in a film.' He looked at their blank faces and explained, 'There are many kinds of films: dramas, documentaries, foreign films.' Seeing that they were still confused, he added: 'It's a bigger world outside. But of course, there aren't so many mountains as there are here.'

As he continued talking, he thought about his school, and about what an oddity he was in the eyes of his classmates: a boy who came from the wild grasslands, five thousand metres above sea level. When he first arrived in Saga, he felt homesick, and often dreamed about the tent that smelt of dung smoke and warm milk, and about the endless, empty plains. In the grasslands, if you have a rifle, some gunpowder, a horse and a dog, you can feed on gazelles and wild deer, and sleep for free under the stars. But after a while, he settled in and began to enjoy the comforts and excitement of modern life. When he left Saga last month and boarded the bus to Mayoumu, he was so torn between the town and the grasslands that he felt as though his body were being ripped in two.

Now, half of his body had returned home. He was sitting in his family's tent on the high plateau near the shores of Lake Drolmula, listening to the wind rustling outside and his family discussing the breeding of yaks and sheep. He knew that the smell of cake in the air was the smell of Dawa's skin.

He stood up, and with his head bowed low circled the tent. He stroked the rough surface of the central pole. As a child, he used to test the knives he made by running the blades through the wood. He stroked the mirror on the door of the wooden wardrobe. Dawa walked over to him and, just as she used to, pushed her head against his. She gazed at her reflection, and he gazed at it too as her hair brushed against his neck. Nothing had changed.

Didn't you want to come home to Mayoumu? he asked himself. Haven't you come home now? Haven't you found your family's tent? Haven't you given Dawa a gold chiffon scarf and a pair of nylon socks, your mother a shirt, a box of powdered orange juice, a scroll painting of a Chinese landscape? But didn't the black horse run away with those presents? You told them that the girls in Saga wear leather shoes and you showed them how they walked. You said: 'I'll take you to Saga. You could find work there. There are books on everything, the roads are as hard as rock, there are a hundred times more shops than there are in Mayoumu. If you go to Saga, you'll never want to come back here again.'

Dawa walked over and poured him some fresh tea. 'Undo your top buttons,' she said. 'You're sweating. Did you meet many girls in the town?'

He stared at Dawa's eyes, then at her mouth, and said, 'The girls in Saga wear jeans, not robes. Their legs are as shiny as yak legs. They take off their jeans before they go to bed. They don't sleep in their robes like us.' After he said this, Dawa looked away, and he too dropped his gaze.

In Saga, whenever he saw a girl walk down the street, his thoughts always returned to the high plateau, and the dank, heavy air that pressed down on it.

Another gust of wind blew on Sonam's face. His

heart sank as he watched the slowly wakening marshes of Lake Drolmula. The ribbons of salt crystals along the shore were soaking up the first rays of the morning sun. The black horse must have delivered my sack to the tent by now, he thought to himself. In a daze, he found himself walking back to his family's tent. The sheepdog Pemu ran up to him and rubbed its head against the zip of his trousers.

Beyond the blue sky he could see Mount Kailash moving towards him. It was shrouded in white clouds, just like Goddess Tadkar Dosangma. He tried to stay upright, but his feet gave way and he collapsed on the ground. A ballpoint pen rolled out from the pocket of his jacket and landed between two blades of grass.

The eight-fanged roach

As the sun turned red, wisps of white cloud drifted towards the horizon. I could tell that the sunset would be beautiful. I checked the view through my camera. There was no snow on the mountains to the east, and the hills in the foreground made an awkward silhouette. I would have to climb the hill for a better shot. I was at the western edge of Tibet's high Changthang Plateau, a region of lakes and hills. It was a good place for photography, but the land was criss-crossed with rivers and streams, and it was easy to get lost. As I crested the hill, the sun dropped below the horizon. In the fading light I scanned the grasslands and discovered that my road back had sunk into the darkness. The rolling plains that spread before me were pitch black, there were no camp-fires in sight. I knew that I'd have to sleep under the stars again. I sat down on a breezy slope and finished the biscuits I'd bought in Baingoin. Then

I dug into my pocket and pulled out two pieces of dried yak cheese that I'd pilfered from a market stall. I popped one into my mouth. At first the taste was so sour that I nearly spat it out, but as the lump softened it produced a milky aftertaste that was comforting and familiar.

Before the night wind started to blow, I spread out my sleeping bag and snuggled inside with my shoes still on. I lay on my back, stared into the black sky and thought about life and death. For Tibetans, death isn't a sad occasion, merely a different phase of life. But it was hard to understand the pilgrims who prostrated themselves for hours outside the temple gates, grating their heads on the ground. Why are men so afraid of retribution? I was hungry. My stomach was empty. A gust of air whirled through my abdomen and slipped out through my guts.

I rolled onto my side to ease the pain in my stomach. It was getting cold. I looked up and checked the direction of the wind, and was relieved to find that it was blowing from east to west. There was a river to the west, and then the flat plains, so that even if any wild dogs over there had caught my scent in the wind, they wouldn't have been able to reach me. I took a dagger from my bag, held it in my palm and lay down to sleep. But as soon as I closed my eyes, I was assailed by terrifying visions:

a wild yak stampeded towards me; a wild dog ran off with my rucksack; a wolf crept up behind me and silently clamped its jaw into my spindly neck; a pack of hungry ghosts surrounded me and gnawed at my ears, nose, hands and feet as though they were chewing radishes.

Then my mind turned to women, and the warm smell inside their bras.

I glanced back in the direction in which I'd come and saw a still, faint light. I reached for my camera, and through the zoom lens discovered that the light was a square air vent at the top of a tent. I hoped that the person inside might let me spend the night there. I climbed out of the sleeping bag and groped my way down the hill. Two hours later, I reached the camp. As I approached the tent, I made a small noise to check whether there were any dogs about. But no dogs leaped out, so I lifted the door curtain and peered inside. An old man was sitting very still by the fire. I greeted him in Tibetan. He turned his head towards me, but couldn't see me clearly at first – he had probably been staring too long at the flames. It wasn't until I sat down by the fire that he realised I was a Han Chinese. He smiled and in Chinese asked me where I was from. I told him that I'd been in the hills taking photographs of the sunset, and that yesterday I had camped in Duoba village. He said that he knew what a camera was. As a young man, he'd spent a few years at Sera Monastery repairing a bronze Buddha, and had seen a few Western and Chinese tourists. He had also been able to pick up some basic Chinese while he was working there.

I put my rucksack down and glanced around the interior of the tent. It was empty. The stones in the fire pit were burned through. It was obviously a popular site for nomads to set up camp. The old man had arrived here that morning, or perhaps the day before. I swept my eyes around the tent again, searching for something to eat, but all I could see were the old sheepskins he was sitting on, a saddle and an aluminium bowl. I asked him if there was any food. He said there was none. I put my hand over the fire. He reached behind him and pulled over some freshly cut wild grass and a pile of twigs. He continued talking to me, but I was too weak with hunger to hold a conversation, so I just grunted occasionally in response. As my mind began to blur, he got up, fastened his belt and walked out into the night. I spread my sleeping bag over one of his sheepskins, crawled inside and closed my eyes.

As I drifted off to sleep, I heard a terrible noise outside. It sounded like a wild beast stamping its hoofs. I sat up, grabbed my knife and lifted the door curtain. The old man was walking towards the tent dragging a yak behind him. He clutched the yak's horn with one hand and put the other over its mouth. The yak struggled to break free. I offered to help, but the old man told me to stay away. He yanked the yak's head down, flicked a knife from his belt and thrust the blade into its neck. Then he whipped off his hat to collect the blood that poured from the wound. The yak kicked and brayed. At last, the old man released his grip, pushed the animal away and watched it stagger back into the darkness. He walked back inside the tent and handed me the hat of blood. 'Drink!' he said, as he returned to his sheepskin rug. He fumbled for a cigarette, lit it, then sucked the blood that dripped from his fingers.

I placed the hat of blood in front of me and watched the steam and froth slowly disappear. I was no longer in a mood to sleep, so I started a conversation with him while we waited for the blood to congeal. He told me that he was a nomad from the pastures near Chiu village. Six months ago, he'd travelled to Shigatse, sold his entire herd of yaks and sheep, and donated the proceeds to Tashilumpo Monastery. I asked what his plans were now, and he said that he was on his way to the Gangdise Mountains to pray to the Buddha, and to wash his sins away in the sacred waters of Lake Mansarobar.

He told me that he had a daughter. I asked him where she was, but he didn't answer me. His eyes darted from left to right. I could tell that he was dying for a drink, so to distract him I took a cigarette from my pocket and tossed it to him.

When he finished telling me his story, I thought of a girl I had seen in Lhasa, and wondered whether I should mention her to him. In the end I decided not to. I was afraid that if I told him about her, he would pester me for more information. And I was also worried that if he'd known what state his daughter was in now, he might have lost his mind. This is what he told me:

'After I sold my herd, I went to Tashilumpo Monastery to pray to the Buddha. I asked the Buddha to protect my daughter, and to allow me to see her again in heaven after I die. I begged the Buddha to help me complete nineteen circuits of Mount Kailash, then allow me to rise to heaven. It was all my fault . . .

'I drank from my mother's breast until the age of fourteen. Her milk never ran dry. My father was killed during the Tibetan Uprising in 1959. The Chiu Pastures are almost deserted now. You will see that for yourself when you travel through them. I was sixteen when I first slept with my mother. Although I saw other women when I went to Chiu village for the annual Sheep Shearing or Yoghurt Festivals, for some reason, I could never break my attachment to my mother. Sometimes she cried about it, but there was nothing we could do. She'd brought me up alone. After my father died, she devoted her life to me and distanced herself from the other nomads. Then one year in Chiu village, I heard that Sera Monastery in Lhasa was recruiting workers to help repair their bronze Buddha. I saw this as a chance to escape from my mother, so I left home and travelled to Lhasa. Our daughter Metok was nine years old by then. If she'd known that she was my mother's child, how could she have lived with herself?

'I learned many things while I was in Sera, but told no one of the sins that I'd committed. Every day after work, I'd prostrate myself before the temple gates to wipe the sins from my soul. But I'd grown used to suckling at my mother's breast, and during those years at the monastery, I chewed my fingers raw.'

I remembered how he'd looked like a greedy child when he sucked the blood from his fingers a few minutes ago. His skin was dark. His dishevelled hair was drawn back from his face and fastened with a purple thread. Red light from the fire danced across the veins protruding from his forehead. He thrust his hands out as he talked, and when he shook his head loose strands of hair swung across his eyes.

'After five years in Lhasa, I thought that my sins had been washed away, so I returned home. Metok was fourteen. I'd bought her some clothes and a pair of felt boots.

'Metok could already weave her own apron by then. Sometimes she'd sit on my lap and let me put up her hair in the Lhasa style. Over the next two years, she grew up a lot, and began to remind me of her mother. In the grasslands, women strip to the waist at midday, you know, just like the men.'

I told him that I'd seen women do this, then I asked him what had happened to his mother.

'She died two years after I returned from Lhasa,' he said. 'When Metok rode with me to the pastures to round up the yaks, the sight of her bare breasts made my heart jump. One day, I lost control. I grabbed hold of a ewe and sucked its udders. Metok saw me do this, and from that day on she kept herself covered at all times and slept as far away from me as she could. I started to drink. I was terrified that my old habits would return.

'Last summer a trader came to our tent asking if we had any leopard skins or antiques to sell. His name was Dondrub. He was well educated, he could speak Chinese. He told us that he'd had a salaried job in Lhasa. But the truth is, he was a very bad man. May he go to hell when he dies! His cart was loaded with goods to sell to the nomads: aluminium pans, plastic teapots, coloured braid . . .'

'Did he fall in love with your daughter?' I said, interrupting him.

'I let him stay in our tent. He put his quilt down next to my daughter, and on that very first night, he slept with her. I could hear Metok groaning softly. It upset me. But part of me wanted Dondrub to marry her and take her away, so that I wouldn't fall into my old ways. That night, I started chewing my fingers again.

'Dondrub stayed with us for two weeks. Every day, Metok served him roast meat and wine. In return, he gave her a hair slide and two plastic bracelets. During the day, I'd stay outside with the animals so that they could be alone together in the tent. But Dondrub's behaviour got worse and worse. Although he wasn't yet thirty, he could swear at women like an old man. If Metok hadn't been so fond of him, I'd have given him a good beating and kicked him out.

'The day before they were due to leave I drank a lot of wine. I should never have drunk so much.' The old man seemed nervous now; he looked at me straight in the eye. The yak blood had congealed.

I scraped it out, passed him the empty hat, then took out my knife, sliced the blood in half and handed him a piece. He took it from me without looking, then with trembling hands scooped it into his mouth.

'It was Dondrub who kept filling my glass,' he said, glancing up at me again.

I had a feeling that he was lying, so I lowered my gaze and stared at the blood in my hand. The light from the fire flickered across the freshly-cut surface of the congealed blood. I could sense that the light bouncing from my knife was darting across his face.

'Dondrub was probably drunk too,' the old man continued. 'I asked him to look after my daughter. I told him that it hadn't been easy bringing her up on my own. He promised that he'd be good to her. But later, when he called me "father", I laughed out loud. I told him that Metok was my mother's child. Metok shrieked when she heard this, and told Dondrub that I was speaking nonsense. But Dondrub seemed excited by what I'd said, and he poured more wine into my cup. I lost all sense of reason after that. I asked Dondrub to let me sleep with Metok. Dondrub agreed, but Metok flew into a rage and started kicking and punching me. Dondrub grabbed hold of her and said, "If you don't sleep with your father tonight, I won't take you away with me." After that, Metok stood still and didn't say a word . . .

'When I woke up the next morning, I found myself lying on top of her. That night I'd released all the frustration that had been building up inside me for so many years. At first I thought it had all been a dream. I went out for a piss, and waited until I was fully awake before I returned to the tent. But when I walked through the door curtain again, I saw Metok jump under a pile of clothes. I ran outside, got on my horse and rode off into the grasslands. When I returned that night, Metok and Dondrub had gone.

'That autumn, I drove my herd to Tsala. I knew that Metok would never call me father again, but I was determined to find her. I asked for news of her in Tsala, but no one had seen her there. Then, in a cart shop, I heard that a month before, a skin trader had passed through the village with a young woman in tow. The shopkeeper asked me whether the woman I was looking for had a turquoise pin in her hair, a round face and slightly puffy eyes. He said that the trader kept swearing at the woman, and spoke in a Shigatse accent. When I heard this, I sold some of my yaks at the market and headed for Shigatse.

'When I reached Shigatse, I was afraid to tell anyone that I was looking for my daughter. Instead, I just asked them if they knew of a man called Dondrub. There were lots of people called Dondrub in Shigatse, but at last I met a skin trader on the street who said he knew the Dondrub I was looking for. He said that he'd gone to Central Tibet to pick up some furniture. I found my way to Dondrub's home, which was twenty kilometres down the road from Shigatse. But when I arrived, Metok wasn't there. I asked Dondrub's mother where she was. I told her that I was a relative of Metok's, and had a letter for her. The old woman said, "You're looking for that little bastard girl, are you? I kicked her out a long time ago. Our family don't mix with scum like her. May the Bodhisattva of Mercy send her to hell!"

'I trekked back to Shigatse, and for days on end I circled the walls of Tashilumpo Monastery, spinning the prayer wheels. The old people I met there talked of a woman not yet twenty years old, who'd slept with every young hooligan in the area. She camped on the streets, apparently, and lived off the donations of passing pilgrims. They said that she came from the Chiu Pastures, and that she'd lost her mind, and would often walk around half-naked. After a few months of living on the streets, her

46

lower body had begun to smell and men were afraid to go near her. The old people felt sorry for her, and said what a terrible father she must have. I was struck with guilt. All day, I threw myself into prostrations, trying to wipe the sins from my body. I begged the Buddha to take pity on me and allow me to find my Metok.'

The old man told me a lot more, but this was about the sum of it. His only wish now was to end his life. He'd heard that many pilgrims who travel to Mount Kailash die while circling its foothills. The more circles they complete before they die, the higher they ascend into heaven. It seemed to make no difference to him whether he returned dead or alive.

I looked up at the smoke vent at the top of the tent, and saw that the square of sky above was already turning white. The yak blood was still lying in my stomach, undigested, and kept sending a nasty, acrid taste to my mouth. I grabbed a clove of raw garlic and munched on it to get rid of the taste. My eyelids were beginning to droop. The old man stretched out on the sheepskins beside me, rested his head on the aluminium basin, and whispered a Buddhist mantra. The tent filled with the smell of his rancid breath.

I lay down next to him, and thought of the girl

I'd seen in the Barkhor market in Lhasa. She had a round face and cheeks blown red by the winds of the high plateau. There was no turquoise pin in her hair. In fact, her hair was so messy it looked like a bundle of yak tails. She kept brushing back the loose strands that fell over her face. When she sensed that someone was looking at her, she would lift her head and smile at them. If they stopped and stared, and didn't throw anything at her, she would stick out her tongue in greeting. The lower lids of her eyes were slightly swollen, but when she smiled, her mouth stretched wide open and her eyes beamed with kindness. It was the smile of the women of the high plateau, a smile as pure as the grassland air. She was smothered by the dust and noise of the crowded street. So that passers-by wouldn't tread on her, she retreated under the table of a yak meat stall. After days of looking up in supplication, her forehead had become lined with wrinkles. Whenever someone stopped and looked down at her with pity, she would drop her head, pull her left breast to her mouth and suck it, then glance up and smile. Her left nipple had been in her mouth for so long that it had become swollen and translucent. As she crouched under the table, stray dogs scuttled about her feet, waiting for scraps of meat to fall from the butcher's tray.

The golden crown

Gar Monastery sat between the goddess mountains Everest and Shishapangma. When I climbed to the highest point of the monastery's compound, I saw these two mountain deities, draped in silver robes, lifting their heads to the sky as though they were yearning to return home. Below the monastery gates ran an ancient horse-trail that was now overgrown with weeds. For centuries, merchants and travellers would pass through here on their way to Nepal. Beside the trail was a winding river that flowed through fields of barley and peas. Beyond the fields spread a dry, stony plain. In the summer months, nomads had to move their herds to graze on greener pastures.

In the past, a bronze stupa that housed a bone of Saint Mileripa had stood at the highest point of the monastery. But all that remained of the stupa now were its grey foundation stones. Many of the surrounding shrines had also crumbled into ruin. The altitude was so high that, over the centuries, the land had become almost deserted. The Tibetans who did still live here were short and stocky, and walked at a very slow pace. Everything that moved: clouds, sheep, dogs, prayer flags, women with children in their arms, and me – a Chinese drifter who'd recently arrived from the east – all did so in slow motion.

My head was pounding. It felt as though a crack had formed around my skull, and that at any moment my crown would lift like the lid of an observatory. Slowly, my memories started to slip away. I forgot what my ex-wife looked like, even though she was the reason that I was leading this sad and vagrant life. I forgot the names of all the important philosophers and writers of the world. Instead, images that for years had been buried deep in my mind suddenly flashed before my eyes. I realised that the keys that I thought I'd lost six years ago were in fact hidden below a wooden chest under my bed. I remembered that when I lost them, I was dreaming of a mouse that was startled by the noise of my keys dropping to the floor. The mouse picked the keys up, unlocked the drawer of my desk, riffled through the contents, took out my bottle of painkillers, swallowed a couple then slid the keys under the wooden chest.

I sat down at a crossroads and gulped deep breaths of air. Children and dogs slowly surrounded me. Some looked at my face and hair, others at my clothes, beard and camera. They squatted down, and in the space between two breaths I smiled at them. Then I stood up, reached into my pocket for my forged introduction letter, and asked for directions to the district headquarters.

The clerk in charge of the headquarters had attended the district high school, but years of working at high altitude had dulled his wits. In the time it took him to smoke a cigarette he read through my introduction letter, then he smiled, and five minutes later, looked up at me. I told him that I had come to climb Mount Everest, that my work unit – such and such publishing house – had sent me here on a political assignment to climb to the summit. He told me that it was impossible to scale the mountain alone. He said that a man had come last year with the same intention, and had even written a will before he'd left, but had returned two weeks later with half his face frozen purple and his nose and ears lost to frostbite. He'd had to spend a month recovering in the district hospital. 'Not everyone can touch the face of the Green Goddess,' the clerk sighed. He told me that at the foot of Mount Everest was an icy river, and that if you slipped into its waters, you'd either freeze to death or be smashed to death by ice boulders. Seeing the dejection on my face, he added, 'But there's a smaller mountain near here that you can climb. From the summit, you can catch a glimpse of Mount Everest. There's a Nepalese monastery up there. It's in ruins now, but there's a small village at the foot of the mountain.'

That afternoon, the district clerk accompanied me to the village below Gar Monastery.

From a distance, it looked like a sheep pen. The stone roofs of the houses almost touched the ground. There was no one about. The ground was so soft and dry that each step I took lifted clouds of dust that hovered in mid-air. A dog crawled out from under a fence and quietly yapped at me. Then a girl's head peeped out from under a stone roof, disappeared into the pit below, and emerged again a few minutes later. She was holding a mirror in one hand this time, and as she combed her hair with the other she stared at me. The path was dusty and scattered with broken stones. The district clerk pointed to a house and said that he knew the owner. 'He's a friend of mine,' he whispered. 'If you give him a packet of cigarettes he'll put you up for the night. He's the oldest man in the district.'

We crouched down, propped our hands on the

stone roof and lowered ourselves into the pit. Apart from the smouldering ashes of the fire, I couldn't see a thing. But I could hear someone sitting in the corner, breathing. I spent the night in this man's home and listened to his story. My head was aching, and the clerk's translation was not always clear, so the account may seem illogical in places. However, the altitude sharpened my awareness for detail, allowing many aspects of the story to remain crystal clear, so I know that I can't have made everything up. What is still a mystery to me, though, is that although the man's story was about a love affair he'd had as a young man, he claimed that the events took place four hundred years ago. This is what he told me:

'At eleven years old, I started an apprenticeship with my teacher – the master craftsman, Sangbucha. Work had just begun on the construction of the bronze stupa at Gar Monastery. My teacher, his wife Kula and I were housed in the monastery compound. I was told that they were both Nepalese, but that my teacher had been born on the Tibetan side of Mount Everest. My father had died of fever while travelling the horse-trail to Nepal. Sangbucha was a very talented silversmith. Almost every woman in the area owned pieces of jewellery that he'd made.

'Sangbucha was employed by the monks to supervise the construction of the stupa. The dome of the stupa was to be cast in bronze and its crown carved from solid gold. I learned everything I know now during the seven years I studied with Sangbucha. His wife Kula was nearly thirty years younger than him. She'd run away from Nepal and moved here to unite with him in a 'false marriage'. When she first met him in her village in Nepal, she was entranced by the beauty of his jewellery. Although she was nearly thirty, her face was free from wrinkles. The sapphire pinned to her nostril was as pure as Lake Mansarobar. Every morning, she would coil her hair into a bun, smear red chalk down her middle parting and dab a dot of crimson cinnabar between her brows. She always wore my teacher's most precious pieces of jewellery.

'The mould for the bronze dome of the stupa took six years to make. The dome was bell-shaped, and was to rest on a stone foundation of tapering steps that at the base would measure four metres in diameter. The edges of each layer of steps were to be decorated with figurines of auspicious animals holding wind-bells in their mouths. Surmounting the bronze dome would be a circular stone platform, from the centre of which would rise a crown carved from pure gold. My teacher told me that the circular platform would keep the rain off the bronze dome below and the thieves off the golden crown above. Thirteen stone peacocks were to decorate the platform's circumference. The stupa would reach sixteen metres high. The crown would be shaped like a miniature stupa, its interior carved with images of the Sixteen Bodhisattvas. Although it would measure just fifty centimetres in length, my teacher's exquisite carvings would render it valuable beyond price. When completed, the crown would be slotted onto the tip of the bronze pillar that would rise through the interior of the stupa.

'I was a strong and conscientious child. I could endure hardship. My teacher liked me very much. He said that the rings I made were better crafted and more beautiful than his. Kula was very affectionate to me, and often put some of my teacher's food aside to give to me later. When I was thirteen, my teacher travelled to Dansang to buy the clay for the mould. He was away for a month. Before he left he asked me to move in to his room. He was afraid that the monks in the monastery would try to sleep with his wife. The first night I spent in the room, Kula told me to lie down beside her. The second night, she leaned over and stroked me. The scent of her skin made me tremble with fear. She smelt of musk from head to toe. A few days later, she invited the monastery's disciplinarian to her room. They waited for me to doze off before they started to embrace, but I was soon woken by Kula's moans. When my teacher returned I didn't have the courage to tell him what had happened.

'My teacher was over sixty years old by then. Although his back was a little bent, he was still in good shape. He had curly hair that fell to his shoulders, and big black eyes. He often wore a purple braid around his head. He didn't drink much, but he liked to flirt with the women who came to buy his jewellery. If a woman took his fancy, he'd add some extra silver to the rings or hairpins he made for them. When he helped a woman put on a necklace or bracelet, he would take his time and stand very close to them.

'The mould for the bronze dome hadn't yet dried the first time I slept with Kula. My teacher was spending all his time locked in his workshop, carving the Bodhisattvas into the golden crown. At night, monks guarded his door to make sure no thieves could enter. Only Kula and the monastery's treasurer were allowed inside the workshop. I was assigned a small group of craftsman and told to supervise the construction work outside. That night, Kula called me to her room. I didn't tremble at all this time. I smiled as I watched her slowly unwrap her sari, then I jumped on her and sucked at her skin as though I was thirsting for drink. From then on, she and I became inseparable. As soon as night fell, I would seek her out, following the smell of musk to her room. Even during the day I could tell where she was just by sniffing the air.

'The morning after we first made love, she travelled to Nilamu to buy some oil and red chalk. In the afternoon, I could smell her coming back. I put down my chisel and rushed to the other side of the mountain to meet her. As I started up the foothills, I saw her coming down. When she caught sight of me, she threw herself on the ground and lifted her sari. We were still rolling on the grass when my teacher turned up. He kicked me hard in the chest, then he picked up a wooden stick and started beating Kula with it.

'For a few days, Kula and I dared not look at one another. We were just waiting for the right time to act.

'Then one morning, Kula burst through my door. Her face was ashen, her eyes were glazed. She stood in front of me and told me that my teacher had left her. He'd run away from the monastery and was never coming back. Later the monks announced that a lot of gold was missing, and that they suspected that my teacher had taken it with him.

I was now put in charge of the entire construction project. The monks were afraid that I too would run away, so they employed a guard to watch over me. I moved into Kula's room. She was kind to me, and told me many stories about her life in Nepal. She wanted me to go back with her to Nepal and become her 'false husband'. She was very home-sick. She told me that she often thought of the day when, as a child of twelve, she had married her true husband: the seed of the sacred cebil tree. She brought out a small parcel and showed me the seed that was wrapped inside. She explained that the seed was invested with divine powers, and that as long as it remained by her side, no harm would come to her. She warned me that when we reached her village she would consult an oracle and that if my astrological signs were found to be incompatible with hers, we would have to separate. She said that her signs conflicted with my teacher's, and that because of this, her family had opposed their marriage, leaving her no choice but to elope with him to Tibet.

'Ten days after my teacher ran away from the monastery, the stupa was finally completed. Kula and I packed our bags and prepared to leave for Nepal. In the evening, she told me that she had spent many hours watching my teacher carve the golden crown and that she knew exactly how to detach it from the stupa. She said, "There's a golden key hidden in a box at the centre of the mandala below the Thousand-handed Bodhisattva of Mercy. To open the box, one must recite the secret mantra *Nam Myoho Renge Kyo* and lift the Bodhisattva of Wisdom. Only the abbot and I know the secret mantra." I considered her proposal for a moment, then told her that I thought it would be too dangerous. I said, "If the monks found out that we'd stolen the crown, we would never make it to Nepal. They might even kill us." But she said that she was certain that her plan would work.

'Late that night, I heard her creep out of bed and leave the room.

'At dawn the next morning, a monk banged on my door and said that Kula was on top of the stupa and couldn't get down. Everyone in the monastery raced up the mountain. Kula had tried to carry out her plan after all. She had managed to dislodge the golden crown, but was now stuck on top of the stupa. Its central bronze pillar was driven between her thighs. She struggled to break free, but as she moved up and down, the pillar grew thicker and thicker until finally she could no longer move at all.

'The golden crown had fallen onto the circular platform. The monks stood rooted to the ground in terror. I fetched a ladder and prepared to climb up, but as soon as it touched the stupa, it burst into flames. I dropped the burning ladder and jumped back. The bronze was as hot as it had been when it was melting in the furnace.

'At last the abbot turned up. He ordered the monks to knock the crown off the platform with a long stick, then he arranged a ritual exorcism to banish the evil spirits. As the invocation was recited, a heavy rain fell from the sky. The stupa became shrouded in thick smoke, but continued to get hotter and hotter. When the rain drops hit the surface of the stupa, they exploded with a terrifying burst.

'Three days later, the smoke finally lifted, and I saw Kula, still stuck on top of the bronze pillar. She was dead now, but her musky fragrance still filled the air.

'The monks and I packed our belongings and prepared to leave the monastery. The abbot said that it was an unsuitable location for a monastery, because it stood on the eye of the Sea Dragon King. He said that the monastery should have been built beside the river at the foot of the mountain. I tried many times to follow the monks down, but the moment I could no longer smell Kula's fragrance in the air, I would fall to the ground.

'In the end, I decided to stay on the mountain and keep watch over her. I moved into the largest room of the abandoned monastery. Sometimes, in the middle of the night, I would hear Kula groan and grunt as though someone were making love to her. After two years on the bronze pillar her body became thin and dry. When the wind blew, she would swing from side to side like a weathercock. When it died, she would always face Nepal, and the horse-trail that runs between the mountain goddesses Everest and Shishapangma. As the years rolled on, her face grew as white as snow and her hair became darker and shinier. Then one day, she finally left the stupa and floated to the ground like a sheet of paper. I walked over, rolled her up and carried her with me down the mountain.'

When he finished telling me the story, he pointed to the wall behind him. 'That's her,' he said. I jumped to my feet to take a look but, because of the lack of oxygen, was soon blinded by a sea of gold stars. Once my vision had cleared, I lit a match and went to touch what was hanging on the wall. It was as hard as dried sheepskin, but the hair was still smooth and glossy. I lit another match, and saw that below the black hair between the thighs there was indeed a large black hole.

The district clerk whispered to me that the old silversmith didn't allow matches to be lit in his room. The next morning I climbed to the top of the mountain. It was just as I described at the beginning – all that remained of the ancient stupa was a mound of loose stones.

As I left the village, the dust that I'd raised the day before was still hanging in mid-air. In front of me, a few girls carrying stones on their backs were walking slowly uphill. After a few steps they stopped to catch their breath, then turned to me and smiled. I recognised one of them as the girl who'd leaned out from under a stone roof the day before and stared at me while combing her hair. Her breasts were very large. I noticed that where the second button was missing, a safety pin tugged her shirt together, faithfully protecting her flesh from view.

The final initiation

The mountain range stretched for hundreds of kilometres, naked and silent under the sun. As dusk approached, the setting rays drenched the slopes in a blood-red light. While the sun sank below the jagged peaks and the last ribbons of light hovered between sky and earth, I started climbing. In those mountains that rose like the ruins of an ancient city, I searched in vain for a pulse of life. The mountains hauled me up, drowned me, then reduced me to an empty carcass. When I could walk no further, I collapsed on the ground, dug my hands into the rocks and sobbed like a child. Then I got up and smiled, and walked back down to the road.

It was the day after I'd left Raga. In my rucksack was a ritual cup, made from a human skull, that I'd bought in a street market. The presence of the skull upset and disturbed me. I had decided to climb those barren mountains to try and clear my thoughts a little and work out what I should be doing with my life. In Tibet, religion permeates every grain of earth. Man and God are inseparable, myth and legend are intertwined. People there have endured sufferings that are beyond the comprehension of the modern world. I am writing down this story now in the hope that I can start to forget it.

She was discovered nine days after the death of the Living Buddha, Tenzin Wangdu. She was just nine days old, but her eyes were wide open and carefully observing the people and objects around her. The shack was built of mud and straw bricks. Light from the butter lamp shone on the frayed cloth of her mother's apron. It was a poor family. When the mother heard the commotion outside, she stuffed the baby back inside her sheepskin cloak. The visitors crammed into the doorway and stood there like a herd of black sheep. The mother got up and invited them in. They were high-ranking monks from Tenpa Monastery. Lama Tsungma, master of rites, headed the group.

Lama Tsungma said, 'We hear that your child was born nine days ago.' The mother confirmed that this was true. The monks instantly clasped their hands in prayer and recited from the scriptures. Lama Tsungma dispatched a messenger to report to his superiors that the new incarnation of the Living Buddha had been found. Then he turned to the mother and said, 'Is it a boy or a girl? What is her name? Sangsang Dolma? Then from now on she will be called Sangsang Tashi.'

A ceremony was held to celebrate the successful reincarnation of Tenzin Wangdu, and Sangsang Tashi's entire family left their shack and moved into Tenpa Monastery.

At fifteen, Sangsang Tashi completed her study of the Five Major Treatises, and began training in Tibetan medicine at Manrinba College. The college was an hour's walk from the monastery. At first, she was driven there in a horse and cart. But after a few months, she requested to walk to the college by herself. She hoped that the solitary excursions would help clear her mind. Feelings that she couldn't describe had begun to trouble her. Until now, all that she had done during the fifteen years of her life was to study Buddhist scriptures and practise yoga.

The path that led to the college gave her great pleasure, and she often dreamed about it in her sleep. She had, however, walked the first part of it thousands of times before. When she opened the door of her meditation room, there it was: a small stone path that wound downhill between the various monastic colleges. At the first turning was a high red wall that enclosed the heart of the monastery: a temple devoted to Sakyamuni and the Sixteen Bodhisattvas. Around this wall was a pilgrim track which one old woman had been circling for twenty years, spinning her handheld prayer wheel, praying that in the next life she would be reborn as a man. Sangsang Tashi often passed her on the way down. Whenever she caught sight of Sangsang Tashi, the old woman would throw herself into a prostration and strike her head on the ground.

Opposite the red wall was the large door to the house of the senior disciplinarian. Stray dogs gathered in the yard outside to chase one another or copulate. Further down on the right one could see the road that led to the monastery's main entrance. During the Unveiling of the Buddha Tapestry Festival, the road filled with hordes of pilgrims. At other times, traders pitched their tents along the side of the road and plied their wares. Between their tents and the small brick houses, beggars and itinerant masons built makeshift huts out of loose stones. Sangsang Tashi often went down to the road to buy bracelets and earrings from the Indian merchants.

When she walked to the medical college, Sangsang Tashi would turn left at the monastery gates, then leave the road and cut across fields of maize and peas. The dwarf willows that lined the path were overgrown with trailing pepperweed. In the morning, the air filled with the scent of wild campions. Sangsang Tashi often stopped on these fields and looked back at the view of Tenpa Monastery. At the top of the monastery compound, halfway up the mountain, was the stone platform on which, during festival time; the Buddha tapestry was displayed. The platform was huge and immaculate. When the wind blew, Sangsang Tashi could hear the prayer flags flapping on the monastery roofs. It sounded as though the cloth were being ripped apart. Hundreds of small shrines hugged the contours of the mountain. Further along the fields, the path crossed a stream that came down from the mountain and flowed into the Nyangchu River that sparkled in the distance.

Whenever Sangsang Tashi walked this path, she forgot that she was a Living Buddha, the reincarnation of Tenzin Wangdu. The scent of the fields intoxicated her. She liked to stand on the wooden bridge above the Nyangchu River and watch the waterweeds swaying in the current. Across the Nyangchu was the medical college, and beyond that lay the bare, desolate mountains.

Tomorrow, Sangsang Tashi would participate in the Ceremony of Empowerment. In this, her final initiation rite, Amitabha, Buddha of Infinite Light, would remove all greed and anger from her heart, and allow her Buddha Nature to manifest itself at last. It was the first day of autumn, and pilgrims were already coming down from the mountain to prepare for the alms-giving that would follow the Ceremony of Empowerment. Sangsang Tashi had no interest in these events. All she wanted was some time on her own to think things through.

Today she arrived as usual for her master's class in the main hall of the medical college. A corpse lay in the centre of the cavernous room. Today the master was going to discuss the location of the subtle body's winds, channels and drops. This was a subject that was of great interest to Sangsang Tashi. Once the novice monks had placed the corpse on the altar, the master picked up his knife. He cut open the corpse's chest, removed the five organs and six innards, pulled out the heart and pointed to the inner eye. The foul stench made Sangsang Tashi nauseous. Although her head was shaved like everyone else, she was the only woman in the room. Beside her stood Geleg Paljor who, like the other ten or so students, was staring intently at the master. Geleg had received the Kalachakra teachings at Panam Monastery, and had been sent to the college to pursue his studies. Sangsang Tashi always liked to stand next to him during class.

The master told the student monks to close their eyes, concentrate their thoughts and try to look into his mind. After a few minutes, four monks said that they had been able to read the master's thoughts. The master asked Sangsang Tashi what she had seen. She was the youngest student in the class, and the only Living Buddha. She immediately entered into a meditative state, but since she had studied yoga for only six years, her inner eye was still clouded. She chanted a mantra to calm her inner deity and regulate her heart channel, but could not visualise the four drops of her subtle body. She felt a sudden burning sensation in her toes. Gradually, the heat became a ball of fire that rose from her legs to her inner eye. She recited the Om Svabhava Mantra to purify her body and steady her consciousness, and slowly saw the image of a frozen river take shape inside her master's mind. Just as her meditation was about to transport her to the Realm of Light, she saw herself standing naked in this river of ice. She swiftly retreated from her trance and told the master what she had seen.

The master said, 'The image you saw in my mind is the image that I saw in yours. The eye that sees the future is not the same as the inner eye.' The master picked up his knife again and rammed it into the corpse's skull.

Sangsang Tashi was confused. The master hadn't explained why she had been standing in the ice river. Was that my future? she wondered. The sight of her naked body surprised her. She looked like a *dakini*, the sky-walking goddesses depicted on the religious paintings she stared at every day. At that moment, the master prised out a small piece of cartilage from below the pituitary gland and said, 'This is the eye of the future. After years of practice, you will be able to use this eye to see the illnesses and evil spirits that hide inside people's bodies. A few minutes ago I saw Sangsang Tashi in the frozen river. This is one of the six sufferings and three austerities she is destined to endure two days from now. But listen to me, Sangsang Tashi – your yogic skills are sufficient for you to keep yourself alive for three days in the ice river without coming to harm.'

Sangsang Tashi felt anxious. The frozen river was far away; she had only ever seen it from the top of a mountain. Although she could sit in the snow for a few days without feeling the cold, she had no idea how it would feel to stand in a frozen river. She thought of the heat she'd felt in her toes a few minutes ago. It hadn't emanated from her own body. She glanced around her and saw a halo of light hovering above Geleg Paljor's head. She smiled at him. She knew that Geleg's yoga had already surpassed the master's, but that he had chosen not to reveal this to anyone.

The master lifted the piece of cartilage from the corpse and said, 'This man was ignorant and foolish. He led a muddled, confused life. That's why the cartilage is yellow. If you achieve enlightenment through meditation, your cartilage will become transparent. The Chan, Orthodox and Tantric Buddhist practices all depend on the use of this eye. It alone allows you to see into the Buddha Realm, clarify your vision and discern the pure essence of all things.'

The master dug out the corpse's eye with his knife and pierced it. Observing the turbid liquid that flowed out, he said, 'The ordinary man sees things through this eye. Because the nature of this eye is clouded, the ordinary man is corrupted by the five poisons and is unable to reach enlightenment.' Sangsang Tashi gazed at the half-dismembered corpse. He was a middle-aged man, with large, white teeth. A swarm of flies hovered above his exposed innards.

In the afternoon, Sangsang Tashi sat alone in her room, meditating. She had just visited her sick mother. Over the past months, Sangsang Tashi had tried to cure her mother's illness with the knowledge she had gained at the medical college, but nothing she'd done had worked. A few weeks ago, she had transferred some of the evil spirits of the disease onto a dog, and the dog had died immediately. But her master had reprimanded her for this. He said that all beings have souls, and that one should think carefully before transferring evil spirits onto other creatures. As she pictured her mother slowly withering away, her mind started to drift once more.

Tomorrow, she would receive her final initiation during the Ceremony of Empowerment. This was the most important ritual the monastery had organised for her since the ceremony that recognised her as a Living Buddha. She preferred not to think about it, though. Over the past days, she had seen the monastic colleges hang new prayer banners in their halls. The long brass horns that had remained in storage for years had been brought out and repaired, and the monks had started practising on them. Every temple was filled with yak butter lamps that were kept alight day and night. Sangsang Tashi continued to stare at the lamp in front of her, but was unable to clear her mind.

She knew that a large ceremonial mandala had been positioned in the centre of the monastery's Meditation Hall. Buddhist figurines and sacrificial offerings, including the washed intestines of the corpse that she had seen dissected a few hours ago, lay on the main altar. Incense burners had been placed at each corner of the square mandala. In front of the mandala were the hard cushions on which Sangsang Tashi would perform the Union of the Two Bodies Ritual. Below the religious wall paintings, hundreds of yak butter lamps had been placed on bolts of red cloth.

The Ceremony of Empowerment was to be conducted as usual by Labrang Chantso. Sangsang Tashi felt short of breath at the thought that tomorrow she would have to perform the Union of the Two Bodies Ritual with him. She sensed that Labrang Chantso disliked her, and that he hated the thought that his elder brother, Tenzin Wangdu, had been reincarnated in her body. But Labrang Chantso was well versed in the secret doctrines. It was he who had instructed her on the Five Major Treatises, and who had conducted her preliminary vase initiation. Sangsang Tashi pictured Labrang Chantso's face. His forehead was lined with wrinkles which crumpled to the side when he looked up. Large black pupils filled his small narrow eyes. He was a tall and heavy man.

Sangsang Tashi thought of the wall painting in the Meditation Hall that showed Bodhisattva Vajrapani, Wielder of the Thunderbolt Sceptre, locked in sexual embrace with his female consort. Tomorrow Sangsang Tashi would have to adopt the consort's position and sit on the Bodhisattva's lap, her legs wrapped around his waist. A hot, damp feeling stirred inside her. Labrang Chantso's face flashed before her eyes. His expression was cold and stern.

She quickly banished these visions from her mind and returned to her meditation, reciting the Sakyamuni Mantra. As she concentrated on the life-supporting wind flowing through her heart, three *dakinis* appeared before her to announce that tomorrow Bodhisattva Vajrapani would take her as his consort. As they disappeared, the *dakini* in the red robe looked back at her and smiled. Then her inner deity, Manjusri, Bodhisattva of Wisdom, appeared in front of her, seated on the square mandala. She felt a heat spread through her body, and the drops of vital energy race through her heart like beads of light. Her stomach, thighs, knee caps and the soles of her feet suddenly became as light as feathers. Then Geleg Paljor's face flashed before her. She felt naked and ashamed, and quickly left the meditation. Her mind was muddled. She tried to visualise herself as her inner deity surrounded by four guardian Bodhisattvas, but failed to see herself within his image. Her head started to buzz, and the noises from outside her room entered her consciousness. She left her meditation once more, and reflected on what the three *dakinis* had told her.

A smell of fried bread blew in through the window. She felt hungry. She banged her wooden fish drum, got her maid to bring her a cup of butter tea and then shut the door. It was night now and the sky was black. Sangsang Tashi stared at the charred wick of her butter lamp and tried to picture how she would look tomorrow. The thought of having to lie down naked in the Meditation Hall made her stomach clench with fear. She tried to wipe this unholy picture from her mind and return to her meditation, but found it impossible to concentrate. She was restless with anxiety. This was the first time in many years that she had been unable to focus her mind. The thought that she was violating her monastic vows frightened her. She relit the lamp that she'd just blown out, recited the Mantra of the Five Bodhisattvas, and at last her mind began to still.

Early the next morning, she woke up and was overcome by the sensation that in every cell of her body, she was a woman. Dawn had not yet broken and a gentle mist still hung in the sky. She felt her blood stream calmly through her veins and her breasts press against her nightshirt. Her thighs, pelvis and stomach felt smooth and supple. As she sat up, she became even more conscious of her femininity.

Then suddenly she remembered that in a few hours she would be lying naked in front of hundreds of people. She wrapped her arms around her shoulders. With her teeth clenched, she stared outside her window and watched the sky turn from purple to blue, then gradually become lighter and lighter.

A crowd of several hundred monks filled the Meditation Hall. Every butter lamp was lit. Bells, horns, drums and cymbals broke into sound. Wearing a ceremonial robe and a necklace of crimson beads, Sangsang Tashi entered the hall, walked to the hard cushions in the middle of the room and sat down opposite Labrang Chantso. She folded her legs in the lotus position, placed her hands on her knees with palms upturned, and chanted the Mantra of the Five Bodhisattvas. Her mind was still agitated, her hands trembled. She felt embarrassed and ashamed. To relieve her tension she dug her feet into the backs of her knees. When the horns sounded again, she realised that she hadn't yet entered her meditation. Quickly she tried to whisper the Tara Mantra to summon her inner deity, but the words came out in the wrong order.

It was too late now. She opened her eyes and saw Labrang Chantso remove his robes and walk towards her. She looked up at him pleadingly then, shaking with fear, let him push her down onto the hard cushions. Very soon, she felt a sharp pain between her legs and the suffocating weight of a body pressing down on her. She sensed that the woman who had woken inside her just a few hours ago was slowly being ripped to shreds.

Soon the pain subsided, and she became aware of the sweat on her back and neck. She let herself roll and shake as Labrang Chantso moved back and forth on top of her. She felt as though she were floating into a black hole. From time to time, an itching sensation spread through her thighs. Inside the black hole, however, she knew that she was alone, and this allowed her a moment of calm.

Then suddenly she remembered that she was performing the Union of the Two Bodies Ritual. She remembered that she must awaken her chakras if she and Labrang Chantso were to achieve a union of wisdom and compassion. But just as her psychic energy was about to reach her Wisdom Chakra, Labrang Chantso dragged her up onto her feet, hitched her right leg to his waist, and shook her so hard that her mind went blank.

She felt herself wither and wilt as Labrang Chantso clung to her like a magnet, sucking the energy from her bones. At last, she collapsed on the floor. She was helpless. She had no choice but to let Labrang Chantso do with her as he wished. When he sat down again in the lotus position and tugged her towards him, she slumped onto his lap and, like the *dakinis* on the murals, hooked her legs around his back. The breasts that had grown on her chest at dawn were now as shrivelled as an old woman's. Sangsang Tashi gasped for breath as the pain below her pubic bone rose through her pelvis and spine.

She opened her eyes. The entire hall was flooded with sunlight. Above the dark clouds of incense smoke that shimmered around her, she saw a golden smile appear on the face of Buddha Sakyamuni. She turned her head from Labrang Chantso's foul-smelling mouth and, among the sea of shaven heads, caught sight of Geleg Paljor. She quickly closed her eyes again, dug her head into Labrang Chantso's chest and clenched her jaw.

It was noon before the Ritual of Empowerment came to an end.

When Sangsang Tashi woke from her sleep, she found herself on the hard cushions, kneeling on all fours like a dog. She was still trembling and soaked in sweat. Her thoughts suddenly turned to her dying mother.

Two nuns walked over, hoisted her up and with water from a golden bowl wiped the blood and sweat from her body. She was paralysed. Her legs were completely numb.

When she finally made it to her feet, the horns blasted in unison and the air filled with incense smoke and the sound of sacred chanting. The golden bowl was placed on the mandala as an offering to the deities. Labrang Chantso had wrapped himself in his robes again and returned to his woven mat. His cheeks were flushed and glowing. Sangsang Tashi's legs shook as she waited for the ceremony to end. She was surprised that in just a few hours she had lost all the yogic skills that had taken her so many years to acquire. But the thought that she was a woman, that in every cell of her body she was a woman, no longer astonished her.

It was on her second night in the frozen river that Sangsang Tashi died. According to the rites, she was meant to meditate in the ice river for three days before manifesting her Buddha Nature. Three lamas had taken it in turns to watch over her and crack the ice that formed around her neck. She had tried to recite an invocation to summon fire into her body, which had proved so effective in the past, but it failed to protect her from the freezing temperatures.

On the third day, just before dawn, Lama Tsungma, master of rites, left the campfire, trod through the snow to the edge of the river and saw Sangsang Tashi's body sinking below the surface. When he pulled her out, he discovered that she had become as transparent as the ice. Where the fish had bitten into her knees, there was not a trace of blood. Her eyes were half-open, as they were when she used to meditate on a flame of light.

At daybreak, a group of lamas arrived to greet the manifested Living Buddha. They were dressed in elaborate ceremonial robes and rode horses draped in coloured silk. It was not important to them whether the Living Buddha was alive or not. Nevertheless, when they saw Sangsang Tashi's body they couldn't help but gather round in amazement. She was lying on her back, frozen to the ice. Cool rays of sun bathed her in a soft light. Everyone stared at the organs floating in her transparent body. A fish that had somehow gnawed its way into her corpse was swimming back and forth through her intestines.

The cup carved from Sangsang Tashi's skull is now sitting on my desk. The man who sold it to me said that he'd inherited it from his great-grandfather who had studied sorcery at Manrinba Medical College. The skull cup used to be Tenpa Monastery's most prized ritual object. It was displayed in the main temple and used only during the most important empowerment ceremonies. The bone has yellowed with age. It must have been dropped at some point in the past as there's a crack down the left side that's crammed with dirt. The fine line running down the dome of the skull zigzags like an electrocardiogram. According to a doctor friend of mine, this indicates that the cranium belonged to a pubescent girl. The exterior of the skull is decorated with ornate brass medallions and the interior is lined with gold.

The seller wanted five hundred yuan for it, but I managed to beat him down to a hundred. If anyone would like to buy it from me, just get in touch. I'll accept any offer, as long as it covers the cost of my travels to the north-east.

Afterword

A hunted animal will always try to run as far away as possible. The further it runs, the safer it feels. In 1985, after three years of running from the authorities in China, I finally headed for Tibet. At the time, the Tibetan Plateau was the most distant and remote place that I could imagine. As my bus left the crowded plains of China and ascended to the clear heights of Tibet, I felt a sense of relief. I hoped that here at last I'd find a refuge from the soulless society that China had become. I wanted to escape into a different landscape and culture, and gain a deeper insight into my Buddhist faith.

But when I reached Lhasa, I found a city that was under siege. The Chinese government, which had 'liberated' Tibet in 1950, was launching celebrations for the twentieth anniversary of the Tibet Autonomous Region. Although the air was filled with the sound of jubilant music, the atmosphere was tense. One could sense the hostility the Tibetans felt towards their Chinese occupiers. No one was allowed out on the streets apart from a select group of people who'd been chosen by the government either to take part in the parades or to stand on the pavement waving flags. On the second night, I couldn't bear being cooped up any longer, and slipped out for a midnight stroll, but was promptly arrested by the local police.

When the siege was lifted, I picked up a job painting propaganda murals outside the local radio station. Once I'd earned enough money, I set off into the countryside. What I encountered both fascinated and bewildered me.

From a distance, the wastes of the high plateau had a hypnotic beauty. But after I had trudged across them for days on end, the emptiness became stupefying. I lost all sense of reality and travelled as though in a trance. In the thin mountain air, it was hard to distinguish fact from fantasy. My mind was tormented by visions of Buddhist deities and memories of home.

In the grasslands I slept under the stars or shared tents with nomads; in the villages I slept on dirt floors. The poverty I saw was worse than anything I'd witnessed in China. My idyll of a simple life lived close to nature was broken when I realised how dehumanising extreme hardship can be. The

Tibetans treated me with either indifference or disdain. Sometimes they even threw stones at me. But the more I saw of Tibet and the damage that Chinese rule had inflicted on the country, the more I understood their anger. For the first time in my life I felt that I was walking through a part of the world where I had no right to be.

My hope of gaining some religious revelation also came to nothing. Tibet was a land whose spiritual heart had been ripped out. Thousands of temples lay in ruins, and the few monasteries that had survived were damaged and defaced. Most of the monks who'd returned to the monasteries seemed to have done so for economic rather than spiritual reasons. The temple gates were guarded by armed policemen, and the walls were daubed with slogans instructing the monks to 'Love the Motherland, love the Communist Party and study Marxist-Leninism'. In this sacred land, it seemed that the Buddha couldn't even save himself, so how could I expect him to save me? As my faith crumbled, a void opened inside me. I felt empty and helpless, as pathetic as a patient who sticks out his tongue and begs his doctor to diagnose what's wrong with him.

I returned to Beijing in a state of nervous exhaustion. I locked myself up in my one-room shack and started writing feverishly. Through the stories that took shape, I wanted to express my confusion and bewilderment, my sympathy for the marginalised and dispossessed, my frustration with blind faith, and my distress at the losses we incur on the march to so-called 'civilisation'. I wanted to write about Tibet as I had experienced it, as both a reality and a state of mind. I let my guard down and wrote without thought of what the repercussions might be.

When the book was finished, I submitted it to Liu Xinwu, the liberal-minded editor of the journal *People's Literature*. Two months later, in February 1987, it appeared in a double issue of the journal. I didn't give the publication much thought because by then I'd moved to Hong Kong and my mind was on other things. One evening, however, I turned on the television and saw a newsclip from Mainland China. The officious announcer cleared her throat and said, '*Stick Out Your Tongue* is a vulgar, obscene book that defames the image of our Tibetan compatriots. Ma Jian fails to depict the great strides the Tibetan people have made in building a united, prosperous and civilised Socialist Tibet. The image of Tibet in this filthy and shameful work has nothing to do with reality, but is instead the product of the author's imagination and his obsessive desire for sex and money . . . No one must be allowed to read this book. All copies of *People's Literature* must be confiscated and destroyed immediately.'

I telephoned my friends in China at once to find out what was going on. Many of them had already been summoned to the police station to be interrogated about me. The editor Liu Xinwu had been sacked from his job, and the official press was filled with articles denouncing my work. A government campaign against the evils of 'bourgeois liberalism' had recently been launched, and I had become its first literary target. The stories' raw descriptions of life went beyond anything that had been published before in China. But by branding it a work of 'pornography', the government had created an interest in the book that they hadn't intended. Soon everyone from college students to taxi drivers became desperate to get their hands on a copy. The journal was sold on the black-market for ten times its issue price. Some entrepreneurs even went to the trouble of making handwritten copies of the book. A month later, the journal *Special Economic Zone Literature* featured another story of mine, and it too was denounced.

I longed to return to Beijing to defend myself against the government's allegations, but my friends told me that I would be thrown into prison and advised me to stay where I was. So I lay low in

Hong Kong and worked on my next novel. The life of an exiled writer didn't agree with me, though. Although I was free to read and write what I wished, I felt isolated and marooned. So when news filtered out the following year that the campaign against 'bourgeois liberalisation' had come to an end, I jumped on the next train to Beijing. I was interrogated at the Chinese border, and then followed to the capital by plainclothes policemen, but no one tried to arrest me. When I approached literary editors with my completed novel, however, I was told that a blanket ban had been placed on all future publication of my work in Mainland China.

In the eighteen years since *Stick Out Your Tongue* was first published, I have returned to China countless times. Sometimes I stay just a few days, sometimes several months. The Tiananmen Massacre of 1989 convinced me that I could never make China my permanent home. Nevertheless, something still keeps pulling me back. I am no longer stopped at the border, or followed by the police. The government doesn't need to keep tabs on me any more, because by denying me a voice they have made me disappear. In China, I have become a moment in history. Whenever I return, I feel like a ghost from the past. On my last visit, I hopped into a taxi near Tiananmen Square. The driver glanced at me through his rear-view mirror and said, 'With hair like that, I guess you work in the arts.' When I told him my name, he said, 'Ma Jian? You wrote that book *Show Me Your Tongue*, didn't you? Yes, yes, I mean *Stick Out Your Tongue*. So what have you been doing since then? Are you still writing books? I thought you were dead!'

I am still writing books, although the only ones that have come out in China have been published under pseudonyms and extensively rewritten by the censors. I am living in London now and, on the surface, my life has changed dramatically. But when I look back at the angry young man who wandered the wilds of Tibet, I realise that I haven't changed that much. I'm still asking myself the same questions, and still searching for a place where I can feel at home.

On the surface, Tibet too has changed greatly, or at least the towns have. Lhasa has become a dirty, polluted city like any other you might find in China, with karaoke bars and massage parlours and gaudy neon signs. The Chinese government has discovered that economic prosperity is more effective than machine-guns and army tanks in silencing demands for democracy or regional autonomy. But the Tibetans who dare question Chinese rule are still treated with the same brutality. Today, over one hundred Tibetans are languishing in Chinese jails because of their political views.

In the West, I have met many people who share the same romantic vision of Tibet that I held before I visited the country. The need to believe in an earthly paradise, a hidden utopia where men live in peace and harmony, seems to run deep among those who are discontented with the modern world. Westerners idealise Tibetans as gentle, godly people untainted by base desires and greed. But in my experience, Tibetans can be as corrupt and brutal as the rest of us. To idealise them is to deny them their humanity.

The Chinese people have retained a very different view of Tibet. For them, it is not a mystical Shangri-La, but a barren outpost of the great Chinese empire. They have swallowed the Communist Party's nationalist propaganda concerning China's 'liberation' of the country, and would fiercely oppose any moves to break up the 'integrity of the Motherland'. They know nothing of the destruction the Chinese have wreaked in Tibet, or of the fact that since 1949, an estimated 1.2 million Tibetans have died due to political persecution, imprisonment, torture and famine.

In China, however, there is a saying: 'That which is united will eventually separate, and that which is separated will eventually reunite.' If one holds this belief, Tibet's eventual separation from China is inevitable. But when and how will it take place? My hope is that the separation will be peaceful and that it will take place soon, before any more of Tibet's unique language, culture and way of life are lost for ever. The Tibetan people, like the Chinese, have been denied control of their destinies, but they are forced to suffer the added torment of being outsiders in their own home.

Ma Jian,
London 2005